Ken Hayes lives with his wife in Bloomington, Indiana. He is a first-time author who attended high school and grew up in Southern California. Sports have always been a passion for Ken. In high school, he played football and ran on the track team. Ken has made a living mostly in the building trades and is currently a painting contractor. His son, Louis, is his partner. Literature was a passion in high school also. And creative writing was always one of his favorite subjects.

I would like to dedicate this book to my son, Louis Hayes, for his advice and support throughout the entire process of bringing this book to print.

Ken Hayes

Run Johnny, Run

AUSTIN MACAULEY PUBLISHERS™

LONDON • CAMBRIDGE • NEW YORK • SHARJAH

Ordering Information
Quantity sales: Special discounts are available on quantity purchases by corporations, associations, and others. For details, contact the publisher at the address below.

Publisher's Cataloging-in-Publication data
Hayes, Ken
Run Johnny, Run

ISBN 9798889107118 (Paperback)
ISBN 9798889107125 (ePub e-book)

Library of Congress Control Number: 2023918110

www.austinmacauley.com/us

First Published 2024
Austin Macauley Publishers LLC
40 Wall Street, 33rd Floor, Suite 3302
New York, NY 10005
USA

mail-usa@austinmacauley.com
+1 (646) 5125767

I would like to acknowledge my wife, Joy Morgan, and my fine friends and members of the Maple Grove Christian Church for making me a better person and author.

Chapter 1

My name is Ralph Dexter and I have quite a story to tell. It begins in a small town in South Dakota. I was sitting in a booth in a little café called the Wagon Wheel. I had finished my breakfast and was drinking coffee and feeling sorry for myself.

About a week ago, I had been fired from my position as head track and field coach at the University of Minnesota. This was, in my opinion, to make room for the dean's nephew. He had been the head track and field coach at the local high school for the past two seasons.

Now I honestly don't think that anyone would consider that he would be qualified to run a program such as the one at the University of Minnesota. And what really gripped me was the way in which I was fired. I was treated like a wayward schoolboy. A member of the school board cited a number of occasions that alcohol was detected on my breath. Well, now I concede that in the past few years I have gotten in to the habit of having a few drinks in the evening when I got home from work. But I never overdo it and I doubt very seriously if anyone could smell it on the breath the next day. I think that it is more likely that a few of my colleagues who have been to my house and joined me for a drink decided to tattle to the dean to gain a point or two.

It was well known that the dean would like to see his nephew hired at my position.

Anyway, that was a week ago. Today I am sitting in a booth at the Wagon Wheel Café in a dusty little town in South Dakota—on a bummer.

I really hadn't decided whether I was happy about the situation or not. Honestly. I had a nice retirement coming from the university and I thought that I needed a change in my life at this point anyway. But right now, all I could think about was the bruised ego part.

I asked the waitress for a check and I noticed that her name was Flo, an appropriate name for a waitress in a small café in a rural town. She smiled and slipped me the bill.

I glanced out the window and took in the ambiance of this small town. It occurred to me that it was like so many towns in America at this point in time, which was 1962. It was right on the cusp between old Middle America and the 20th century. This end of town was still unpaved and the shops along the street were all one-story clapboard buildings. It reminded me of the town I grew up in—Sioux City, Iowa.

Just then something caught my attention and I started hearing a high-pitched noise. When I turned and looked across the street, I saw a puzzling scene. A young girl seemed to be the source of the high-pitched sound. She was hanging over the rear wheel of an old horse drawn buckboard—in a very precarious position.

I kicked myself out of the funk that I was in and I headed for the door with as much speed as I could muster. But my foot had fallen asleep and I stumbled as I reached the door. With bells clanging, I yanked the door open and rushed outside and caught myself right before I did a face plant.

As I looked to my right, I noticed a young man racing up the street. He was running towards the little girl in distress but he was moving at a decidedly higher rate of speed and with much more grace than me. He had long black hair which was trailing behind him as he ran. It was quite a picture and although I kept moving myself, I could not help but notice just how fast he was moving. My mind was concentrating on getting to the little girl as fast as possible, but I could not help but get the feeling that this boy was moving faster than anyone I had ever seen before.

As he approached the rear of the buckboard, he took one final step and launched himself up on to the back end. He gently lifted her from her precarious position. He then motioned to me with the tilt of his head and handed the girl down to me.

Flew up on to the buckboard might be a more accurate description. I accepted her carefully and took her over to the curb and set her down.

Just then, the girl's parents came out of the general store and ran to the young girl. As the mother consoled the child, the father extended his hand to me to thank me. I turned around to the young man to explain that he was really responsible for rescuing the girl. But he was gone. Wow! That was quick. He had vanished so fast that it gave me an odd feeling. Almost as if I had encountered something or someone supernatural. Extraordinary to say the least.

I strolled back across the street to the café and slid back in to the booth where I was seated. Flo was soon over and she asked me if I wanted another cup of coffee. She asked me what the commotion was about outside. I explained to her the predicament that the little girl was in and how a young man had come running up the street to rescue her. I further explained to her my amazement at the young boy with the long black hair and how he ran like the wind and virtually flew up on to the buckboard to save the girl.

"That was Johnny," Flo said with an affectionate grin. "Johnny is always doing things like that. He works out at the saw mill and lives on the reservation with his mother and five young brothers and sisters." "It's kind of a sad story," she further explained. "Johnny is well known around town for his big heart and his heroics." She recounted a number of unbelievable acts that Johnny had been responsible for over the years, one of which she had witnessed herself.

Then Flo took on a strangely, almost angry demeanor. She told me how in recent years some of the men around town tormented Johnny. Out of jealousy or just the mean side of human nature, some men had taken to staging false situations for Johnny. Then they would howl with laughter when Johnny came running because he thought someone needed help. The cruelest part was that Johnny continued to fall for the pranks because he couldn't bear the thought that it might be real. It was not his naivety or innocence that they preyed upon but simply his sheer goodness.

I noticed that Flo was visibly upset at recounting her story about Johnny and I might have detected a tear in her eye. She brushed it away feigning that it was just something in her eye or a flaw in her mascara. But it only reinforced the feeling that I had earlier that something extraordinary was going on here.

Chapter 2

I resumed my journey to I'm not sure where, south on highway 83. I knew that I was going to visit a coach and close friend of mine at the University of Texas. And I think I was going to end up settling somewhere near my sister in Florida. She lives just north of the keys.

My sister and I are very close and her husband and I get along very well. John and I are, I guess, what you would call kindred spirits. We share a lot of the same passions in life. I really have never known anyone who can make me laugh as much as John does on a regular basis.

John owns a small boat repair business. And he does really well. He is well hooked up with a lot of boat maintenance and boat manufacturing companies on the east coast of Florida. I have never told anyone, not even John, that I had entertained the thought of doing the boat bum thing. John had introduced me to many guys he knew who were making a killing doing boat repair and maintenance. It seemed like a pretty laid back and lucrative lifestyle.

Anyway, almost everything that I owned was packed in to this old Oldsmobile. I guess I thought that I would just head in the general direction that I was going. How's that for a master plan?

I knew that my sister would take the news hard that I had been fired. Probably harder than I did myself. If I know John, he'll just laugh and say, "Come on down and we'll go fishin'." That's what I like about John.

It feels so strange for someone like me who has lived such a stable, reliable, predictable, well, you get the picture, way of life. To find myself so free feels kinda weird to say the least. But good.

I pulled in to a gas station and checked my watch. About 4:30. I got some change when I paid for the gas and I called my friend Ted Jensen.

"Hi Ted. It's Ralph," I said. "Hey listen. Are you sitting down? No, it's not real bad news. Well, I guess it's bad news honestly. I was fired the other day from my job at the university."

"Ya, Ted. No, it's alright. Ya, I'm fine, Ted, but hey listen. I'm on the road in South Dakota and I was wondering if it would be alright if I came and visited you for a day or two. How's the timing?"

"Great. Well, I'm going to drive for a few hours and then stop at a motel for the night. Then I'll get up in the morning and drive all day and stay at another motel. And so on 'til I get there. Near as I can figure, I should make it to the university by Saturday."

"How's that sound? No, Ted, I'm fine. Just got a bruised ego, I suppose. The director pulled a shitty on me to get his nephew in. You know, you met him that time at the convention in Houston," I said.

"Ya, the crew cut. Ya that's him. Ya, he is a good coach. But not ready to coach at the university level," I added with emphasis. Ted agreed.

"But listen, the bottom line is that I feel good about it. Really. I'm going to stop by and visit you. Then I'm going on down and visit my sister in Florida. Maybe end of living there," I said.

"No Ted, I really don't need a shoulder to cry on. I'm really alright with it. I admit that my pride is hurt but I think it is the best thing for me," I added as believably as I could sound.

"And just think about it. How many times are we going to get to visit with no agenda? Oh, and Ted, have I got a wild story to tell you about what happened to me in this small town this morning?" I said. "Ya, I'll tell ya all about it when I get there. OK, Ted, see ya, and thanks." I got off the phone with Ted and I felt a little relieved. It was not going to be easy to explain to people about losing my position. Folks like my sister were not going to understand. To tell you the truth, I was a little surprised at how lightly I was taking it. I suppose that should tell me that I was a little more than unhappy in my position and I didn't even realize it.

When I got back out on the road, I pushed the Oldsmobubble up to speed. The old boat was cumbersome around town but it was the greatest out on the open road.

As I settled in to the task of the road, I thought back to the events earlier in the day. How completely strange and unique the whole thing was! It still echoed in my mind. I just couldn't stop thinking about the speed at which the young man was moving and the height that he obtained when he jumped up in to the buckboard.

Now I know that people do amazing things when adrenaline is racing in their veins. And there are many stories about women lifting cars off their children. But I had a feeling that this was different. And further, I am a professional track and field coach and I have seen some of the greatest athletes compete for many years. I even attended the 1960 Summer Olympics in Rome, Italy. In fact, it was one of the high points in my life. But what I saw today simply amazed me.

The young man could possibly be one of the greatest athletes of all times. There I said it. Or thought it anyway. So now what do I do about it. That's a very good question. It would be different if I was a track coach at a major university. Like I was a week ago.

Then I would try to recruit this young man with all my might.

But now I am a retired track and field coach. How ironic!

So how was I going to just forget about it? But what should I do? What could I do? Call up my replacement at the University of Minnesota and make my replacement a hero? I'm not that noble. And I'm not feeling very loyal at this time. I could let my friend Ted recruit him and then they would kick Minnesota's ass for the next few years.

Orrrrrrrrr… I could coach the boy myself and be ready for the next summer Olympics coming in 1964, which was to be held in two years.

Now most everyone would just say, "That's nuts." But they had not seen the boy in action. But what was right for the boy and his family. Why was I even thinking this way? At this point, my mind was going a mile a minute. All questions. No answers. And as far as ironic goes, this was indeed a dusey.

I passed a billboard that said, '*Twenty-six miles to the Murphy Motel. Just $8 a night.*' I'll get cleaned up and get a good night's sleep and maybe put my thoughts in better prospective tomorrow.

Chapter 3

OK, so much for a fresh perspective tomorrow. As I got back out on the road, I headed south. I realized that I had no fresh perspective at all. So, it didn't surprise me when I pulled over and made a U-turn.

I must say that it had a calming effect on me that I had made the decision. If nothing else, I could at least explain to Johnny some of the options he had if I was right about his ability.

I pulled in to the same parking place that I had occupied yesterday. Flo was making the rounds with a coffee pot. "Hey mister, you a regular now," she said when she spotted me. "Just didn't get enough o' that top notch coffee," I quipped. "And I'll be honest with you, Flo. I wanted to talk to you about something. About that young man that I saw yesterday, Johnny," I said. "I was formerly the head track and field coach at the University of Minnesota and I think that the young man could have high potential in sport of track and field."

"I'll be glad to help you, mister. What did you say your name was? Well, I guess you didn't say your name," she said.

"My name is Ralph Dexter," I said. "And your name is Flo as I see on your name plate."

"Yes," she replied. "So, you got an eyeful yesterday," Flo said knowingly. "Ya, there have been a few who tried to get Johnny in to sports. The problem is that his father died a few years back and Johnny had to quit school to support his mother and his five younger brothers and sisters. He takes his job real serious," Flo said seriously.

"But if you're bound and determined to talk to him, you can catch up to him out at the lumber mill. That's where he works. They take lunch from 12 to 12:30 in the parking lot," she said. "Just go out o' town on highway 83 north for about two miles and go left at Grand Fork and you can't miss it."

I thanked Flo and finished my breakfast. Then I sat for a while and thought about what I was going to say to Johnny. Quite a while.

I pulled the Cutlass in to the dusty parking lot at about 12:10. I got some angry stares from some of the men who were sitting on their tailgates. As the cloud of dust ascended upon them from my old car.

As I set the brake, I looked over and saw Johnny sitting on the tailgate of his truck, swinging his legs. I noticed that all the men were sitting on their tailgates or in their cars in twos and threes and fours. Johnny was sitting alone.

"Hi," I said. "My name is Ralph Dexter. I saw you yesterday when you rescued that little girl." Johnny shook my hand and said nothing.

"Listen," I said, feeling uncomfortable already. "I would like to talk to you about something that could be very important to you and to your family. I was formerly the head track and field coach at the University of Minnesota. I am no longer in that position but in seeing you in action yesterday, I got the idea that you might have some real potential in the sport of track and field."

I let Johnny think about that for a while. Then he took a long pull on his root beer and he looked at me and said, "I'm not interested, mister."

Well, let's just say I wasn't ready for that. He wasn't rude. Just firm. And all of a sudden, it occurred to me that I wasn't the first one to recognize Johnny's potential. I felt like a salesman trying to sell ice cubes to Eskimos.

"Well, think about it," I finally said. "I'll be around for a few days." I got in my car and left to a chorus of mean stares. I got the distinct impression that these were not the sensitive brand of males.

Chapter 4

I went back in to town and I rented a motel room for the night. Then I called my friend Ted and explained to him that I would be delayed a day or two. And I told him about my meeting with Johnny. I had been known as a very good judge of talent in my years of coaching at the university. Ted knew that well and was very interested in what I told him about Johnny.

After settling in to my room, I clicked on the TV and a soap opera was on. Well, after about ten minutes, I got so depressed that I turned it off and just laid on the bed, staring at the ceiling.

I took a short nap and when I awoke, it was three o'clock. I locked my room and strolled over to the Wagon Wheel.

"Hi stranger," Flo greeted me. "So, you a regular now. How'd it go with Johnny?"

"Not so good," I replied. "Johnny simply said that he wasn't interested."

"Well, I coulda toll ya that," Flo drawled. "Johnny's dead set on taking care of his family. That's really all he's interested in. That boy has never had anything on his mind but taking care of his family. Or caring for anyone else in need that should come along. If you don't appeal to that mindset, you ain't never going to get anywhere with Johnny."

"What you need to do is to talk to Johnny's mother. Johnny's not going to look at anything but doing what's best for taking care of his family. His mother, on the other hand, will see a broader picture," she said with emphasis.

"Wow, thank you so much for that insight, Flo," I said.

"Would you like some lunch," she offered.

"Yes, I would. Do you have any blueberry pie?" I said.

"Best in the county, if not the country," Flo said with pride.

"Thank you for all the help, Flo. I really appreciate it," I said.

"No problem," she said dismissively. Then she looked back and said to me, "I think that you mean to do some good for that boy and I'm all for that. I have known him since he was a child and let me tell you; I have a real soft spot for him. I'd love to see him make a name for himself. And a better life for his family. And I know he could."

I took in the ambiance of the small-town lunch crowd. A couple of farmers in bib overalls. A family with two small children and an older boy sat at another table. They all seemed happy and well fed.

Flo came back with my check and she laid a piece of paper next to it.

"Here's the address and directions to the Bureau of Indian Affairs. They will be able to give you directions to Johnny's house," she said.

"Do you think Johnny would be mad at me for talking to his mother?" I asked.

"Well," Flo said calmly. "Johnny doesn't get mad. But I think it would be alright if you went and talked to his mom. You can say you talked to me."

I crossed the street and entered the general store. I figured that I might need a notebook and a pen when I talked to Johnny's mother. Just if I needed contact numbers or to take some information down or whatever.

I left town and followed the directions that Flo gave me to the Bureau of Indian Affairs. The office was a little brick building about ten miles out of town.

As I entered, the woman behind the desk said,

"Hello, what can I do for you?"

"Hi, my name is Ralph Dexter," I replied. "I am a retired track and field coach at the University of Minnesota. What I need is to get the address of a young man who lives here on the reservation by the name of Johnny. I would like to talk to his mother about an opportunity for Johnny."

"Well, Mr. Dexter, that would be Johnny White," she replied. "I could help you but let me ask you a few questions. You say that you are not a friend of Johnny's but you just observed him. Is that correct? And you would like to talk to his mother, who you have not met about his future. Do I have it right?" she said.

"Yes Ma'am," I replied.

"Well, let me do this," she said. "I will call Johnny's mother and I will tell her what you said and we'll see if she is interested in talking to you. We'll go from there. I would be all for helping anyone who lives here on the reservation for there are so few opportunities available."

"Great," I said as I sat in a chair and the woman left the room.

The girl seemed nice enough. I could only hope now that she would relay my message in the proper context. I knew that if Johnny's mother would not talk to me, I would have to just forget it, no matter what my instincts told me about Johnny.

Chapter 5

It was all set. The young woman at the Bureau of Indian Affairs had talked to Johnny's mother. She had been very excited to talk to me about what the woman said. She gave me the directions to Johnny's house and said that I was welcome to come to their house and talk to her tomorrow morning at 10 a.m.

The next morning, I was prompt and the directions were good. Johnny and his family lived a few miles off the main road. There were small one-story houses scattered around the area where Johnny lived. Not a tree in sight.

I pulled the Cutlass in to the driveway and was greeted by three small children with long black hair. Like Johnny's. I was then greeted by, and I might add, a striking middle-aged woman who introduced herself as Terry.

"Hello," I said. "My name is Ralph Dexter."

"Please come in," she offered. "Would you like a cup of tea?"

"Yes please," I said. "That would be nice."

The children were left to play outside, as it seemed they had been instructed to do for our meeting. I was thankful for that, as I am not very good with children. Never having any myself. I loved them dearly but I just wasn't comfortable around them, and children can sense that.

Terry returned with a pot of tea and the fixings.

"So," she said, "you wanted to talk to me about something to do with Johnny and sports."

"Yes," I said. "I have recently retired from coaching at the University of Minnesota where I was the head track and field coach. And I don't know if your son told you or not but I observed him the other day when he rescued a little girl in distress. And I observed a super-high degree of athleticism and I would like for him to consider pursuing his ability in track and field."

There was quiet. I could tell that she was thinking about what I had said. Finally, she said, "Mister Dexter, I don't know if you are aware but Johnny is the sole breadwinner for this family since his father died a few years ago."

"Yes," I said. "And by the way, I was told that by a waitress at the Wagon Wheel café in town. And by the way, she has a very high regard for your son. Her name is Flo."

"Well, I am very well acquainted with her and I will have to thank her the next time that I see her," she said.

"Mister Dexter," Terry continued, "I don't know if you are aware but Johnny has many gifts. His compassion and gentle nature are apparent as you have witnessed yourself. I am also aware of his gift for running and agility. But Johnny also has a way with animals that few people have. It is as if he can communicate with them on their level. Many have witnessed this and in fact Johnny is well known around here for his talent working with and training horses.

"Mister Dexter," Terry continued after a sip of tea, "I am very aware of the talents and natural abilities of my son. And let me tell you that I am more than ashamed and saddened that he feels that he must support us since his father died. I receive compensation from the government since his father died but if it wasn't for Johnny working as hard as he does, we would not live as comfortably as we do. Johnny's father was a full-blooded Lakota Indian. And he was a very proud man. Johnny is very proud like his father. And very stubborn like his father. And they are both very dead set against taking anything that they did not earn.

"So let me tell you a little about Johnny, as you will need to understand him some if you want to help him in any capacity. My son is a very unusual person. He is completely devoted to his family. He is 100% selfless. He has never in his entire life wanted anything for himself. I can hardly get him to buy himself a pair of shoes, Mister Dexter," Terry said as she shook her head.

"In fact, Johnny's love for running started when he was in about the third grade. The school that he attended had very limited transportation. They offered any family a small check per month if they would provide transportation for their own children to and from school. Johnny would run to and home from school each day so that the family would get a little bit of money each month. It was seven miles each way.

"The program ended after about a year but Johnny kept doing it until he quit school in his sophomore year to go to work. Mister Dexter, let me say that Johnny is such a good son that I feel honored to be his mother," Terry said as she looked me right in the eye.

There was another one of those quiet periods and I could tell that Terry was deep in thought.

"Mister Dexter, I don't know if you are aware but some people around here do not appreciate Johnny's abilities or his goodness," she said.

I could see a shroud of sadness pass over her face.

"Some of the men here in town play horrible tricks on Johnny. But he endures all the tricks and ridicule. I don't know how he does it," she said plainly. "There was an occasion a few years ago that a group of boys played a horrible trick on Johnny. They talked a little girl into telling Johnny that her cousin was trapped in the basement of a cabin high up a nearby mountain range.

"There was a lot of snow on the ground. Even down here. Johnny drove his jeep up to the base of the mountain and hiked up a dangerous trail to get to the cabin. When he got to the cabin, he broke the lock on the basement door and got sprayed by skunks who had been living in the basement.

"Johnny just came home, took a vinegar bath, and lived in the shed for a couple weeks. He didn't even tell me what had happened. I only found out about it when I overheard some of the men bragging about what they had done. All Johnny cared about was that everyone was alright. That's just the way he is," she said again, looking me right in the eye.

Chapter 6

I could tell that it was my turn to talk as Terry grew silent. "Well," I said, "I am not currently in a position to directly set Johnny up with a university program. I am however very well connected to the universities and athletic powers in this country. And I might add that if Johnny is as good as I think he might be, we could possibly consider the Olympics in track and field. What I propose to do is to give Johnny a few simple running tests to determine his level of ability. And then advise him on his possibilities," I said.

Just then, the door flew open and two children raced to Terry's side, pronouncing innocence in some altercation with the other. Her answer was that both children would forfeit dessert following supper if she was to hear another word about it. So simple. So ingenious. A talented mother could be one of the wisest people in the world. The bickering ended immediately and both children went outside without another word.

"So, Mister Dexter," she said after the door was closed. "I hear what you are saying but I will tell you right now. It will not be easy convincing my son to consider your generous offer. But I will put it to him like this. You would like to give him a few simple running tests to determine his level of ability. Is that correct."

"Yes," I said. "That would be a good way to put it." I continued, "Let me write down the number at the motel that I am staying at. You talk it over with Johnny and give me a call one way or the other. I will plan on staying in town for a few days and I will look forward to hearing from you."

Terry said, "OK." And I headed for the door.

"Mister Dexter," Terry said, "between you and me, I am going to try my hardest to get Johnny to consider your offer."

"Thank you," I said. And I left.

Chapter 7

The next day passed with no word from Johnny or his mother. I was very firm in my conviction that if I did not hear from them in the next two days, I would then go on my way and forget all about it—somehow.

The call came the next evening as I was returning from my supper at the Wagon Wheel. The man at the desk at the motel that I was staying called to me as I was returning.

"There is a call for you, Mister Dexter," he said.

"Hello," I said. "This is Mister Dexter."

"Hello this is Terry," she said in a timid voice. "I have talked to my son and he has agreed to let you test him."

"Well, that's a very good news," I said. "Will tomorrow be OK? Say about one o'clock."

"That will be fine," she said.

"I trust your son will be able to guide us to a nearby high school track," I said.

"Yes," she said. "And when you come tomorrow, he will be ready to go."

"OK," I said. "And thank you for your help."

"You're very welcome, Mister Dexter," she said.

And we hung up the phone.

The next day was a balmy day as a weather system seemed to be moving in. I had my fingers crossed as it seemed that Johnny would not need much of an excuse to cancel our meeting.

As I pulled the Cutlass up to Johnny's house, I was greeted by the same greeting party as the day before. But this time, they seemed a bit apprehensive. This alerted me to the possibility that some heated conversations had taken place between Johnny and his mother.

"Hello," I said as I approached. "I am very pleased that you have consented to this test." Johnny and his mother shook my hand and they appeared to be in good spirits.

As Johnny got in the car, I said, "Do you have any shorts or lighter tennis shoes?"

"No sir," he replied. "Just these shoes and jeans." I looked at Johnny's pf flyer high top tennis shoes and frowned.

"OK, it will have to do, I suppose," I said.

Johnny gave me directions and the rest of the trip was made in silence. That seemed to be Johnny's specialty. And I certainly wasn't the chattiest guy around.

"Turn left up ahead," Johnny finally said. "It's about a mile down." As we pulled in the parking lot of the high school, I could see that it was indeed a regulation track. That would be very helpful in determining Johnny's time in relation to current standards.

"Why don't you get warmed up a bit?" I said. At that, I went to my trunk and got out my stopwatch. The feel of it was comfortable and familiar. That's when it occurred to me that I was going to miss coaching.

Johnny was oblivious to proper methods of stretching before a workout, which should not have surprised me at all. "Here Johnny, let me show you some basic stretching and warm-up exercises," I said.

After a good stretch, I told Johnny to just jog around the track real slow. I took a seat in the bleachers and watched as he ambled around the track. The first thing that I noticed about his gait was that there was no wasted motion. Very fluid. I have coached so many athletes who have developed so many bad habits that are so intrinsic that it is almost impossible to overcome them. There was no way that I would need to break Johnny of any bad habits or instruct him on his running form. It was indeed the most perfect form that I had ever seen.

"Slow it down," I called out to Johnny. "This is just a warm-up." I was beginning to realize that although Johnny had great talent and ability, I would have to work with Johnny and start him at Square A. As a coach at the university level, I was not used to this.

But I was sure that I could do it.

As I looked at Johnny and his high-top tennis shoes, I made the choice to have him run a quarter of a mile on the inside of the track on the grass. It would not be a genuine quarter but it would be close enough to get a good idea of Johnny's speed. As he finished his jog around the track, I waved him over as I approached the track.

"Johnny," I said. "I would like for you to start here on the grass on the inside of the track and run around the track one time. Fast. Don't go crazy but run pretty fast so that I can get a good idea of your ability."

"I am going to time your run with this stop watch, so wait until I say go before you start. OK?"

"OK," Johnny said and he stood where I had pointed and waited for me to say 'go.' He didn't shake his legs and he had no special look on his face.

"Go," I said, and Johnny took off like a shot. I thought, *Oh no, I've blown it already.* I forgot to tell him to pace himself. A quarter mile run is at a fairly high pace but still it is not considered a sprint. Johnny started around the track at almost a sprint pace. I was just hoping that he wouldn't hurt himself.

It was a sight to behold. As Johnny passed the 220 yard or eighth-mile marker, he was already below most high school records for that distance. And he still had another 220 to go.

As I look back on that day, I still have no way to put into words how I felt to watch him run that day. Let's just say that I had never seen anything like it. I knew that I had been right immediately. And then as Johnny rounded the second curve, I thought that he would surely fold. I remember at the time; I was really worried, not by how he looked but by the blistering pace that he was keeping.

Then Johnny did something so surprising that I almost dropped the stopwatch from my limp hand. As Johnny finished the curve and started down the straightaway, he started what is known in the business as a kick. And I mean it was some kick. He simply put his head down a little and he almost flew to the finish line. How did he know how to do that?

As I stared at the stopwatch, I could not believe what I was seeing. I had just seen it and I knew it was fast. But WOW! Johnny had run on the inside of the track which would have taken a few yards off the distance but his time was very near a world record.

And if that doesn't catch your attention, Johnny wasn't even winded. Even the best athletes show distress after such a run. I could hardly believe it. I didn't know what to say to Johnny so I just said, "Nice run."

Funny thing was, I had a sneaking suspicion that he could have shaved a few seconds off the time if someone had been in distress.

I had planned on timing Johnny on some other distances but I changed my mind. I knew what I needed to know and it was best to error on the safe side after a run like that. So, we loaded up and headed back to Johnny's house.

Chapter 8

I had to gather my thoughts now as the Cutlass purred down the highway. Johnny was quiet but it appeared that he was always quiet. What was different was that I was quiet. I really wasn't prepared to be quite so right. It was time to present to Johnny and his mother the undisputable truth. Johnny is world-class fast.

As we pulled up to Johnny's house, we received the same welcoming committee as before. And this time they seemed to be happy and perhaps caught up in the mood of anticipation. Johnny gave attention to each of his siblings in equal time, I noted.

"Can I have a word with you and your mother?" I said.

"Sure," Johnny replied as he entered the house. "Make yourself at home. I'll find my mother." A few minutes later, they both emerged. Johnny's mother smiled and extended her hand to me and she asked, "How did he do?"

"Well, Mrs. White, Johnny did exceptionally well. Let me put it to you this way. I have no doubt whatsoever that with a minimum amount of training in track and field, Johnny could be a threat to quite a few of the existing world records in the sport of track and field. His time today was within seconds of the world record. That is with no training and without proper equipment. This is what I suspected and now I have proof that I was right," I said.

"Well," Johnny said, "I really appreciate what you are trying to do and it does sound like a good opportunity but it is most important to me to take care of my family."

Terry looked away at that point and I could see tears well up in her eyes. When she turned around, she blurted out to Johnny, "You do not need to do this. I can manage with your father's pension and government aid. It is just for a while and we would manage."

She looked embarrassed that she had spoken so loudly and Johnny just looked down. I could tell that his mother did not regularly raise her voice. It was written on both their faces.

"Mother," Johnny finally said, "I would love to do what Mister Dexter proposed for me. I would love to do well like he says that I can and do better for you and the young ones. But will they have the best shoes while I am gone and will you have the things that you need. Or will you all go without while I am away trying to make it better for us."

"You know," I said during a period of silence. "I am ready to go all in on this. I say right now that I can afford to take care of Johnny's room and board and food during this process plus help with the family while Johnny is away if needed. It would mean a lot to me. I would think of it as an investment. I am not a rich man but I am willing to invest in Johnny's future. He will need a coach to help him train and to navigate the system. I am prepared to invest in his future because I believe he can be successful. His success can bring financial rewards. Currently in the Olympics there is no financial reward directly for competing but endorsements of products by athletes are starting to pay some large amounts. Plus, there are pro sports teams that would love to have Johnny on their roster." Johnny looked at his mother and spoke, "I know what you say may be true and you and the young ones would get by but let me ask you this. What would father say if he was here and knew that I was turning away from my responsibility to the family and my promise to him?"

Terry's reply was slow and I was surprised at how patient and mild her temper had become.

She said slowly, "I think your father would do what he thought would be the best for the family as you would, my son. I think that if your father had the gifts to do what you can do and he knew it would enrich our future, he would do it. But he could not. Your father was a good man but he was not unique like you are Johnny. You must think of what you can do to make it better for our family, not just OK."

Terry looked right in to Johnny's eyes as she said this. I could not have said it any better myself. In fact, I knew that I could not have said it so well.

"And yes," said Johnny, "that is why I am considering the offer that Mister Dexter here proposes."

Ooooooooooooh. That was news to my ears. He was considering my offer. I really had no indication before this that Johnny was considering my offer. I felt lighter.

Terry looked at Johnny with tears in her eyes. Johnny just looked down and nervously played with a small toy on the coffee table.

"You know," I said after a silence. "I am going back to my room. I would love for you two to talk about this and then call me at the motel and let me know what you would like to do. The offer stands no matter how you would like to proceed." I shook hands with Johnny, and when I went to shake hands with Terry, she gave me a big hug and whispered in my ear, "Thank you."

Chapter 9

As I settled in on my drive back into town, I reflected. My first feeling was a sense of relief. Johnny was going for it. But what I did not expect was the effect of the responsibility that I had taken on.

I must admit that I have not had a lot of responsibility for others in my life. Never married. No children. What if the plan did not work? I would be letting Johnny and his family down. But if it did work, Johnny could help himself and his family very much. The weight seemed to be in my consciousness. So, I put it aside.

I knew that my first stop must be to drop by the diner and let Flo know the good news. I must have had a king-sized possum grin on my face. Flo knew right away that the news was good, so I was met with a king-sized hug.

"Tell me all about it," Flo beamed. So, I gave her the rundown. How Johnny's mother was the reason Johnny had agreed to go with me, which was Flo's advice, so I thanked her and gave her another hug.

Next, I went to a phone booth and called my friend Ted.

"Ted. Hi it's Ralph. I have some good news. You know the young Indian boy that I was telling you about. He has agreed to go with me and train," I said.

"No Ted, I'm still fired. I am just going to train him in hopes that he would qualify for the next Olympics in Tokyo. Oh yeah, there are a million questions that I don't have answers for but when you see this young man run you will know why I must do it," I said.

"Ya actually, I'm going to pick Johnny up tomorrow morning and we'll hit the road. Oh yeah, still got the old boat. She's the greatest out on the open road. We will stay in motels on the way and as we get closer, I'll give ya a call and let ya know our progress and when to expect us. I figure it will take three or four days. I won't push it. Ya, you know me Ted, my night vision isn't that good. OK, OK. Oh really. Wow, that would be super. Ted are you sure that would be no imposition. OK, see ya soon," I said and I hung up.

Ted had offered us a place to stay. It was only about twelve miles to the university. Evidently, it was an old hunter's cabin that Ted owned that had sat empty for a couple of years due to a small issue that he had not gotten around to taking care of.

I was thrilled at the prospect of sharing this adventure with my best friend. Ted and I had known each other since high school. We had shared many hopes and dreams throughout the years. I just hoped that this endeavor would let us have another great memory after all was said and done.

45

Chapter 10

So tomorrow morning became this morning. I pulled up to Johnny's house to the obligatory greeting party which was Johnny's brothers and sisters. Today they seemed especially jubilant, which changed dramatically when they saw Johnny coming out of the house with his suitcase. Then there came a period of wailing and crying that would have woken the dead. If there were any dead around! The younger ones were consoled by the older ones who were also close to tears.

But just being brave.

OK, so here I go again. Now I was breaking up a family. And again, came the self-doubts. I had laid out a basic plan the night before. I was to drive in daylight hours only, making it to the next town each day with enough time to secure a nice room for that evening. Then proceeding the next day. Sounded like the standard road trip.

Our first stop for the night will probably be North Platte, Nebraska. Johnny and I settled in for our journey into the fantastic future.

Now my old car cruises the road as well as any car ever made—in my opinion. But… the seats were not anything that you would describe as comfortable. They were hard and torturous—to be honest. So, after a few hours spent in silence, which was a constant in Johnny's nature, I offered Johnny to use the back seat to stretch out and relax or sleep. Johnny just shook his head no. In fact, to my surprise, Johnny sat in the front seat for the entire journey, eyes glued to the road ahead.

Now if I had known Johnny better at the time, this would not have surprised me. He did not want me to have to drive alone. He was there to support me. In his mind, I think.

Let me explain something to the reader at this point. I only had an inkling of who Johnny was. And for a long time, he seemed very complicated to me. But later and after getting to know Johnny better, I came to realize that Johnny was the most predictable person there could be. Just think what someone would do in every circumstance if they were:

Number One: completely honestNumber Two: completely honorable

Number Three: completely unselfishNumber Four: unafraid of any consequences in the pursuit of helping someone else in need.

Chapter 11

We had been driving for about four or five hours when I pulled in to a gas station. At the far end of the parking lot, I saw a young girl sitting on a large trunk. She had long, blond hair and was dressed very colorfully. This was a sight that you did not often see here in Corn Land—Nebraska.

Johnny and I got out of the car and stretched our legs. The young woman spotted Johnny and made a beeline towards him. Now I need to mention at this point that Johnny is not an unattractive young man. He has long, jet-black hair and distinctive cheekbones and hawk-brown eyes. And let me add that this young woman was not without extra good looks either.

It was my guess that she was a hippie. She wore a tie dye tee shirt and she had a flower in her hair. A dead giveaway.

"Check under the hood, mister," the attendant said. "Please," I told him. And at that point, I went in to the nearby store to get some snacks. When I came out, the young lady and Johnny were over by her trunk. I sauntered over and introduced myself.

"Hello, my name is Ralph Dexter," I said.

"My name is Kathy Murphy," the young girl said as she shook my hand.

The first thing that I noticed about the girl was the incessant smacking of her gum, done with her mouth half open. But I could not help but notice how beautiful she was, although a little less so with the smacking of the gum—in my opinion.

Now as it turned out, Kathy—bless her heart—had been dumped here by her free-spirited, fun-loving, hippie boyfriend. She had talked Johnny into asking me for a ride. She didn't seem to have a particular destination. I asked her if she wanted to go back home. She just said, "Hell no." So, I said, "Welcome aboard."

Kathy produced a fresh $100 dollar bill. She gave it to me and said, "This is for gas."

I said, "That's not necessary." But I took the bill and I stuck it in my pocket.

It was a tight fit to get the young lady's trunk in the trunk of car but did make it. Now let me suffice to say. It never crossed my mind or Johnny's, I'm sure, to leave this beautiful young girl out in the middle of nowhere—Corn Land, Nebraska, by herself, many miles from home, wherever her home was.

Chapter 12

Kathy made herself at home in the back seat with a number of colorful knickknacks and battered notebooks. After a few miles, it started. Kathy talked constantly. The funny thing was that it did not matter what anyone said. That is if you perceived a slight opportunity to speak. It did not alter her conversation, which was always about HER.

"Do you ever give it a rest?" I finally replied.

"Well, it seems that I have to talk enough to make up for you two logs in the front seat," she snapped.

"And by the way," she added, "what's up with you, old man? Rollin' with Cochise here. What are you guys up to? You're an odd pair if you don't mind my saying so."

Although I did not feel that I owed our passenger any explanation, I said, "I am a retired track and field coach and Johnny and I are going to the University of Texas to train."

"Train for what?" she said.

"Running events," I said. "Johnny seems to have an extremely high ability."

Kathy thought about this for a minute. Then she said, "So you can fly, huh, Cochise."

"My name is Johnny," he said firmly but softly.

"So can I," she said. "And as a matter of fact, it was the only thing that I was really good at in school." As the trip went on, I will admit that Kathy's chatter did bother me a bit. She talked constantly.

Johnny seemed to listen intently though. He was very patient with her, as I might guess a lot of people would just tune her out. I know I did. But Johnny listened and seemed to show interest in the odd assortment of topics she discussed.

She told us about her idea that someday she would start a commune in her friend's back yard, which was 10,000 acres, she said. All the people at the commune would work together to raise all the food they would need. Now the only form of monetary value to be used was marbles. And you could gain marbles by only two methods. One, win them in a fair game of marbles with another member of the commune. Or two, you could receive them from the leader of the commune, which was HER. The marbles would be given for acts of unselfishness, heroism, or kindness.

Now the thing that really surprised me about this idea of hers was that her friend's parents were alright with it. She assured me that they were.

Chapter 13

Now Kathy, unlike Johnny, had no compunction about stretching out or sleeping in the back seat. When her jaw muscles finally got tired, she went fast asleep. And that girl can snore. Let me tell ya. It sounded like a freight train, fully loaded, running up a steep grade.

It was one o' those funny but it-ain't-funny deals.

We were approaching North Platte, Nebraska. So, I pulled into a gas station. Kathy awoke, startled, evidently forgetting where she was at first.

Now I might mention at this point that this young lady, although very self-absorbed, was very polite and respectful. I would venture to guess, spoiled but well brought up.

I received advice from the gas station attendant as to a good motel in town. We drove over to the motel he had suggested and I approached the desk. As I approached the desk, I was surprised to see Kathy next to me. "I've got this," I said. "It's all part of my investment in Johnny's future," I added.

"I'll take care of my own responsibilities if you don't mind, Ralph," she said. And at that, she opened up her little grab bag and it was filled with $100 dollar bills. And peanut shells and candy wrappers etc. But it was hard not to notice that it was a LARGE amount of money.

Johnny and I settled in to our room and Kathy settled in to hers. There was a diner just a short walk from our room. We all agreed to get something to eat, then come back to the room and get cleaned up and relax. So, at the diner again, Kathy paid her own tab and that is how it went.

After supper, Johnny and Kathy went to an arcade nearby while I stayed behind and read the newspaper. The year was 1962 and Americans were pretty happy for the most part. Shows like *Ozzie and Harriet* were on the television in black and white and they set an impossibly high standard of how a family should operate. One son writes hit songs like, **"Hello Mary Lou,"** while the other son is just the model older brother. Mom cooks and cleans the house all day in preparation for her husband to return home from work. Of course, like I said, it was an impossibly high standard to follow.

I didn't know anyone like the Nelson's.

I was starting to read the world news again since I wasn't in any rush to get back to the room when Kathy burst through the door and said, "Come and look at this, Ralph. It'll blow your mind." So, I followed Kathy to the arcade. Johnny was busy on a pinball machine and lights were flashing and alarms were sounding as the points were tallied on the display.

"He said he's never played pinball before and look at that score," Kathy said as she pointed to Johnny's score. "And it's only the third game that he has played."

Sure enough. Kathy was right. As I watched Johnny's hands on the flippers, it seemed like he controlled the trajectory of the steel ball with a master's touch. The precision with which the ball always hit the target, never getting out of his control, was innate.

Chapter 14

The next day, back out on the road, all that Kathy could talk about was how Johnny had played the pinball game. "He's a wizard," she kept saying. "Maybe he's got some special powers handed down to him. You know that Indian mojo stuff's awful strong. I have heard."

And that was pretty much the conversation for the entire day.

Johnny, of course, didn't comment unless he was asked a direct question by either Kathy or myself. What I realized somewhere along the way was that Johnny and I were happier because of Kathy and her quirky nature. It just seemed to me that she brought something out in Johnny. It allowed him to be himself more. I hadn't seen much of his personality. It was almost as if (before Kathy) he was afraid to show it. Now I could tell he had a wonderful sense of humor and a truly special way about himself that I would have never guessed.

So, I seemed to enter the conversation less and less as the two got to know each other better. And it was entertaining. Of course, Johnny didn't talk much but there were times that Kathy demanded as answer from him. He always carefully considered the question that was posed and always had an interesting answer, to tell you the truth. Kathy was a real sweet kid. And it was apparent that the two were falling for each other. Polar opposites as they were. But they had one thing in common. They both loved to RUN. That was interesting.

I figured that our next stop would be in Kansas. If you ever want to drive for a long time on completely flat, mostly straight roads, then drive through this part of the country. Between Kansas and Nebraska, I must say, there is no more monotonous landscape on the planet. Now if you are from or live in this part of the country, then I apologize to you. But I don't take it back.

As the conversations continued, which I might add, never stopped for the entire journey, that is if Kathy was awake, we all got to know each other better. I am thankful to her because I was learning more about Johnny, more than I would have known without her assistance.

I also got a glimpse into the mind of a young woman, which seemed to be a strange and wondrous place, filled with fantasies and dreams that I could have never imagined.

It was about three o'clock and we were about 40 miles out of Garden City, Kansas. I figured it to be our next stop and it was a good thing because Kathy was running out of things to talk about. I was wrong. It was just an uncharacteristic lull. She immediately embarked on a new journey, of which I do not recall. There were so many.

Chapter 15

Garden City was a little larger than most of the towns that we passed. It was my idea to go to a market and get some fresh fruit and vegetables and sandwich meat and bread for dinner. We all agreed. We chose a tidy-looking motel, walking distance to a food store and pulled in. The same routine was followed as the previous night. This time, we could not get an adjoining room for Kathy, which was alright with me. The thin walls of last night's room did little to keep out the sound of the approaching freight train, which was Kathy.

I have lived much of my life alone, so I really don't know if I snore much. I don't think I do. Johnny seemed to not snore at all.

It was an uneventful evening spent watching television and munching on fruit and snacks that I had purchased at the little market.

The next morning, we got out on the road early. The weather had taken a turn. It was dreary and a bit foggy. We would soon be going through the panhandle of Oklahoma. It was cooler than the previous days and it was a welcome change.

The conversation today seemed to take a shift.

There was a lot less mindless chatter coming from Kathy. She was more inquisitive as to Johnny's past and even mine, which I did not mind sharing. The topics were much less about herself and she seemed to have a genuine interest in the two logs in the front seat, which was her earlier classification for Johnny and me. She opened up and shared a little of her own background, which I will share with the reader at this time.

The first revelation was that she openly admitted to being a spoiled rich kid. She had been raised by her nanny since childhood. And the family maid whom she adored completely. Her mother and her father gave her all that money can buy—but little else.

They were both accomplished business executives and their jobs occupied much of their time. Kathy inherited a large amount of money when her grandmother passed away. Not like it is usually done in a trust fund that you receive at a certain age or an annuity. No. Kathy said she got her inheritance at age 17 in a lump sum. Just plop! She did not say how large that sum was but I got the impression that it was LARGE.

Not long after she graduated from high school, she met a boy who promised her the world. They traveled around the country in his van for a few months until it became apparent that this boy was more interested in Kathy's money than in Kathy. So, when she refused to make aforesaid money available to him, she was deposited by the side of the road, which it was not long after that Johnny and I came along.

Chapter 16

As we ventured into Texas, the towns had a different look altogether—dustier. I had studied the map the night before and it looked like Abilene might be a good destination for the day. That is why I had us get an early start. This would be the longest leg of the journey. From Abilene to Austin would be the shortest. It also seemed like a good idea because the day was a bit cooler and the old Cutlass did not have air-conditioning.

Texas certainly had a lot more interesting scenery, not anything that you would call pretty but more interesting, I suppose.

The conversations were not as in depth or constant as before. I think that we were all a bit more involved in our own thoughts about the future that lay ahead of us. Kathy had voiced the request that she go all the way to Austin with us. She had heard that it was a beautiful college town and somewhere that she would like to visit. So, I said that she was welcome to come along and that we would help her make arrangements for a place to stay when we arrived.

I had called Ted that morning and informed him of our progress. I judged we would be making it to his house in Austin tomorrow—sometime in the afternoon.

We stayed in a motel in Abilene, Texas, that night. Abilene, I must say, was nothing like I pictured it would be. There were no cowboys sleeping outside saloons on dusty streets. And there were no clean and convenient motels to be found either. It was not a good part of town where we finally decided to stay. Unfriendly people and bad food was all that I remember about Abilene.

Now if you are from that town or currently live in that town, then I apologize to you. But I don't take it back.

Chapter 17

I think that I might have bald a tire as we left the motel. Kathy and Johnny felt the same way and we had a good laugh. Kathy even drew caricatures of the desk clerk in her notebooks. They were not very flattering. I found them to be very good. She had definitely caught the man's utter disgust for his fellow man in his features.

We were again back to a hotter day, so it was not as comfortable as the day before. So today, the conversation was a lot more about what lay ahead in Austin. I had only been to Austin on one occasion for a track meet. I didn't really know much about the town. And I didn't know anything about the cabin that Ted had offered for us to stay in when we got there. We would have to just get there and see.

We pulled in to Ted's driveway and were immediately greeted by his Irish wolfhound. Ted came out of the front door with the broadest grin on his face. I introduced him to Johnny first, then Kathy. Ted and I hugged like only true best friends do when they haven't seen each other in a while.

"Come on in," Ted said. "You must be hungry and weary. I've got some of my homemade chicken and dumplins on the stove. Want some coffee yaaawl?" Ted drawled. "No thanks," Johnny replied, kinda flinching at Ted's accent.

"You bet," I said.

"How 'bout you, young lady?" Ted said to Kathy.

"Yes please," Kathy said politely.

"Well, ain't she a pretty thing?" Ted said to me as we lagged behind, entering the house.

Ted had a very neat and well-appointed house. He had definitely done better for himself than me. We had both been head track coaches at universities for about the same amount of time. I kind of felt a little pang of guilt that I had not done better for myself financially.

All I owned was that old car.

Ted made us feel right at home as only an old country boy can do. We sat around his coffee table and chatted over some old times and fresh coffee. Then came the chicken and dumplings—some of the best that I have ever had.

Next, we retired to Ted's living room. I laid out our plans to Ted as best I could, not having a very good idea of what the plan was actually. Ted said that we could bed down in the main house for the evening and he would show us the cabin at daybreak.

Kathy seemed resolved to let the boys talk and figure things out. It was a very nice evening and a pleasant change from motels and the open road.

Chapter 18

The next morning, we awoke to a glorious day.

From what I could see off Ted's back deck, Austin was quite nice. I could see rolling hills and a lake nearby. I could even see the university off in the distance.

Ted cooked up a tasty breakfast of eggs and ham for us. Then we packed up our bags and followed him to the cabin. Ted's cabin was not as little as I anticipated. It was actually a nice little two-bedroom house. I guess Ted called it a cabin because it had rustic surroundings with no houses nearby. It was about a quarter of a mile to the nearest house.

Ted informed me that he had a plumber come by and fix the issue that he had told me about, so we were all ready to go. I offered to pay for the repair but he wouldn't have it. It was just something that needed to be done, he said.

The place was pretty well furnished. Nothing fancy.

But everything we needed. Kathy claimed her bedroom. First thing, I had not even considered that she would be staying with us. I think she never considered not staying with us. We had just become the three musketeers, it seemed.

Ted and I took the opportunity to talk logistics. He gave me his schedule and the best times for access to the track and facilities. He would even afford us a locker in the main building and Johnny could use the showers after workouts.

It seems that Ted had a much better relationship with management here than I did back in Minnesota.

The facilities were nicer and his office made mine look like a broom closet. And yet my accomplishments over the years were certainly a match for his—only saying.

After Ted gave me the rundown, we said goodbye. Kathy and Johnny thanked him profusely for his generosity.

"So, I'll flip ya for the other bedroom," I said to Johnny. "No, you take the bedroom, Ralph," Johnny said. "I'll take the couch. It's what I'm used to."

"OK, I said," a little relieved. I didn't want to sleep on the couch. I've had some back issues over the years and I didn't want to chance it.

"Now if you have any issues with the couch, you be sure and let me know. OK Johnny," I said. "Your physical health is very important to me as you know."

So we settled in that evening to our new abode. Ted had stocked the kitchen for a few days. Now all that I knew how to cook was TV dinners and something simple like a steak. As it turned out, Johnny was a pretty good cook. Kathy couldn't boil water. She told me that she had never cooked anything in her entire life. When you are raised with a fulltime maid, I guess that is the result.

Johnny said that he had always helped his mother cook for the family. And he enjoyed cooking. I felt a little guilty, I suppose, but not enough to learn how to cook.

Kathy just figured that someone else would do the cooking. So, Johnny was our cook.

After supper, we were sitting around the small dining room table talking. I pulled a fresh one-dollar bill out of my wallet and I said to Kathy, "I bet you can't catch this dollar bill when I drop it."

"Oh yeah," she said. "Just watch me."

It was a little thing that I have done many times over the years and it amazed people every time. You hold up a bill with your index finger and thumb and you have someone then hold their finger and thumb halfway down the bill but not touching it. Then you drop it. They are supposed to catch it. Seems easy, huh. I have done the exercise many times with many people and no one has ever caught it. I never have either. The lesson being that gravity gets things going a lot faster than you ever imagined.

So as expected, Kathy did not catch the bill.

"Try it again," she challenged.

"OK," I said. We tried it four times. I saw it at the same time as Kathy did. Just a little smirk at the edge of Johnny's mouth.

"OK, smarty pants, you try it," Kathy said to Johnny.

"OK," Johnny said. So, I held up the bill and Johnny got ready and after a long while, I dropped the bill. Johnny caught it. Then he handed it to me.

Chapter 19

Alright. So, I suppose that I was getting used to these little surprises from Johnny. But they were still a surprise. Maybe someday I would get used to it. But I wasn't there yet.

As I lay in bed that night, thinking about it, I had a funny thought. It was almost as if the good lord used a completely different mold for Johnny as he did for the rest of us. He was by far the most unique person that I had ever met—and for that matter that I had ever heard of.

The following day, we headed in to town to pick up some groceries. I would also get Johnny some workout gear. Kathy picked out most of the groceries. Evidently, she couldn't cook. But she could shop. But then I guess that comes natural to all women. No offense, all women.

We then went to a sporting goods store to pick up some gear for Johnny. I figured that I would wait and talk to Ted as to where to get the best set of cleats for

Johnny. Good cleats are an important tool for a track athlete.

Kathy picked up some games and books. She wanted to go back to the cabin and have some alone time. After we took her home, Johnny and I headed to the university. I was looking forward to working with Johnny and it seems that he was looking forward to it also.

Ted was going to stop by and take a look at Johnny.

As far as being on the track, we wanted to be there when the student athletes were not. So, we had a window today of 11 a.m. to 1 p.m. I would just start Johnny off with some wind sprints after a good stretch. With wind sprints, you run 100 yards on the grass, then you rest for just a couple of minutes and run the 100 yards the other way, not at a full sprint but at a pretty good clip.

Johnny had completed a few repetitions when Ted appeared. So, I told Johnny, "I want you to kick it up a notch so that Ted can see what you got."

Now this was only the second time that I had seen Johnny run. That is other than the day I first saw him. And I had not seen him all out at a sprint distance. He had run a quarter mile before. It is a very different race compared to the 100-yard or 100-meter race.

Johnny toed the line and Ted said, "Go." About five seconds later, Ted knew exactly what I was talking about. And I realized that Johnny was not only a world-class middle-distance runner but a world-class sprinter as well. This is rare in the world of track and field. Sure, some middle-distance runners are fast. And some sprinters are fast at middle distance. But world record threatening at both, it was unheard of.

Ted was blown away like I knew he would be. "My gosh, Ralph! When you said fast, you weren't a woofin'."

"And you oughta see him in the quarter," I said.

"He's that kinda fast in the quarter too," Ted said, dumbfounded.

"Yes," I said.

"OK, Ralph, I know exactly what you are talking about now and count me in. I'll help in any way I can. That young man is special alright. That's the fastest that I have ever seen a human being run."

"Me too," I said. Then Ted walked away, shaking his head.

"How you feelin', Johnny," I said.

"Good, Ralph," he said. "What did Ted think?"

"He was quite impressed and so was I," I told Johnny.

"Let's do a few more reps and we'll wrap it up."

Chapter 20

So, after a few more reps, I motioned Johnny over to the stands and we had a seat.

"Johnny," I started, "it seems that I was completely right about your potential. I will just say bluntly to you that you may very well be the fastest runner that the world has yet seen.

"Now that comes with a great responsibility to myself and to you. I certainly make no promises but I think we are on the right course. And I think that we should proceed," I said.

"OK," Johnny said, shaking his head yes in agreement.

"So go hit the showers and I'll see if Coach Ted is in his office, OK?" I said to Johnny as I patted him on the back.

Ted was at his desk, so I knocked lightly and entered his office.

"Well, you really got yourself something special there, Ralph," he said. "I'd give up all I got to coach that boy," Ted said, looking right at me.

"I know," I said. "And I really appreciate your help."

"Don't mention it. I'll just feel blessed to be a part of it," Ted said flatly.

"I'm not exactly sure that I know how to proceed."

I said, "I know what all the basics will be, of course, workouts. Training with the starting blocks. Getting used to the track and the track cleats. But it will need to be a different approach with someone who is already so naturally fast."

"I know what ya mean," replied Ted. "But that's a pretty good problem to have, eh." And he nudged me in the ribs.

"Ya, I ain't complainin'," I said with a grin.

We saw Johnny appear from the locker room, so I said goodbye and thanks to Ted.

"See ya!" Johnny yelled to Ted as we departed.

Chapter 21

With coach Ted's advice, I purchased Johnny a good pair of running cleats. The best that they make, Ted assured me. We settled in to a training regimen and I taught Johnny the use of the starting blocks and we started some of our training on the track at actual competitive distances. Johnny never shied away from the hard work of training. As a matter of fact, he always seemed disappointed when the workout was over. It was very apparent that Johnny loved to run. Of course, if I was that fast, I would probably love to run too.

As time went on there was a growing fan club in the stands whenever Johnny was working out. And Ted was receiving some backlash and questions from some of the staff at the university. It seems that they had no problem with a friend of Ted's training at their facility. And they were aware of my credentials. But they were getting wind of Johnny's talent and they didn't know how they felt about that. Evidently, a little bird had told them that Johnny was so fast that he could smoke any of their athletes. They did not understand why Johnny wasn't pursued with a scholarship offer Ted had offered. You can bet on that. But Johnny would have none of it. He would be away from his family for too long. And there was also the fact that Johnny had quit high school in his sophomore year. I just hoped that they would not renege on their offer to let Johnny train here. It was a perfect set up and I did not have a Plan B.

Chapter 22

The three musketeers settled in to the business of running a household. I got a phone installed and we purchased a few items for the kitchen and the rest of the house.

We also were getting to know our way around the university and the town of Austin. What a neat little town Austin is! We all just fell in love with the town and the people in the town.

The city of Austin had a thriving music scene. Johnny and Kathy would borrow the Oldsmobubble some evenings and go catch some bands and live music downtown. They never consumed any alcohol as far as I know. They were a good influence on me as I did like alcohol. A bit. OK, a bit too much. But since the three musketeers got together, I haven't touched a drop. And given how good these two kids were, I sure didn't want to be a bad influence.

I had put off calling my sister long enough. I really dreaded it. John would probably have to peel her off the ceiling when I told her that I had been fired. And I was living in my friend's cabin in Texas, training an Indian boy to compete in the Olympics. There was no way to sugar coat it.

So, I finally called her. And yeah. It was bad. She cried like a baby and threatened to jump in her car right that minute and come and straighten me out. I must have contracted some form of temporary insanity as she put it.

Kathy bought a little used Volkswagen bug. You would see her and Johnny tooling around town usually with her at the helm.

I always think it looks funny to see folks in a bug, especially if they are fairly tall or real tall. Now Johnny is about 6'1" and Kathy is about 5'10". To me, they look comical driving around with their heads almost touching the roof.

Kathy had made a few girlfriends as of late. A nice little hippie girl who worked at a boutique that Kathy frequented.

Johnny and I were continuing to train. The weather was getting cooler and winter was upon us so we did some training indoors. But for the most part we reduced the training by quite a bit through the winter. Of course, this was not Minnesota, so there were many days of outdoor training that we could do. We worked on general fitness and resistance exercises. I found out that Johnny is very strong. I mean VERY strong. I do not believe in weight training for a track athlete so we did not do any weights.

Johnny called his mother frequently and I offered many times to send money if she needed anything. She flatly refused and insisted that they had all that they needed.

At Christmas, Johnny and Kathy sent all kinds of presents to the kids. I sent a few myself. And one special present to Johnny's mother. I might add that I was very smitten by Johnny's mother. I rate her as the most attractive and dynamic woman that I have ever known. I even fantasized about a relationship with Terry. I would never do anything about it though. I am kind of a coward when it comes to women. But I sent her the most beautiful dress that Kathy, Johnny and I could find. I had a feeling that things were going to change for Johnny and his family in the next couple of years. Terry might need to have something special to wear at the awards occasions that I figured were to come.

Chapter 23

As spring sprung in 1963, Johnny and I started training more rigorously. Then one day, Kathy showed up at the track in full running gear. She intended on training with Johnny.

By the way, at this point the two of them were in a romantic relationship and were totally committed to each other. So now I had two athletes to train. I was feeling a little more like a coach now. Kathy took my advice very seriously from the beginning and was a very good student and learned fast and listened well.

They ran together a lot but there were times that I worked on her skills exclusively. Kathy did not have the blazing speed that Johnny had and seemed to be more fitted to the longer races, possibly the 880 yard or the mile.

As we continued to train, it became apparent that neither Johnny nor Kathy liked putting in a lot of miles in training. They both found it boring. But Kathy was really showing an aptitude for the 880. So much so that after two months of training, I asked Ted to take a look.

We both agreed that she had potential, so Ted introduced her to the head coach for the women's track and field team at the university.

Thelma was her name and she saw Kathy's potential immediately. Kathy then started training with the girls' team.

A scholarship was discussed for the following year, as the current semester was already underway. She would not be able to actually compete in the upcoming outdoor season.

Kathy made the commitment to her coach and became a very diligent track athlete. She would attend the university the following semester, scholarship or not.

That is when I found out what I had suspected all along, scholarship or not. Kathy could fund four years at the university, no problem. Maybe she could buy the university if she wanted to. Her fortune was in the millions. And she made no bones about helping any friends with that power of money if needed. She did not flaunt this fact with Johnny and me but it was understood that she would commit her money to good use if needed.

Johnny of course was steadfast against allowing her to buy anything for him. Even where there were times that he really needed something she would almost have to beat him in the head to get him to take it.

Chapter 24

The three of us were attending indoor track meets and Johnny and Kathy were really becoming great students of the sport.

Johnny was making great progress with his start in the 100 meters. Starting blocks are a learned art and the first part of the race is something that does not come as natural as high-end speed. But Johnny was improving.

There was absolutely nothing for Johnny to learn in the 400 meters. I had already let him completely cut it loose on the track with cleats and he had come just five tenths of a second under the world record. Let me tell ya it's something to witness such a thing. Just Johnny and I there. Well, let me correct that statement. The janitor was there doing some clean-up in the stands. I thought he was gonna fall over. It's just a good thing that he had his broom to catch himself.

Johnny was also making progress on the long jump. The long jump is a real learning process. You will never be good at it if you're not extremely fast already.

But. It really takes some time to get your steps down and the takeoff and the landing. There is a lot to it.

Most athletes make a mark part way down the runway. As you pass that point, the left or right toe is supposed to land at that mark if you are on pace. You adjust your mark as you experiment with your approach. You should have maximum speed right before the last three steps that you take. The last three steps are a little shorter. Your take off foot should land flat footed to give you maximum height for the jump.

That will allow you to gain more distance with the jump.

And the landing. That's another thing. You are supposed to land on your butt. But your feet land first. Stretched out as far as you can. Then when your feet touch, you actually push down and pull yourself in that last instant as far as you can before your butt touches. It ain't easy. But Johnny was starting to get some great jumps. Not record threatening in the least but good jumps. As I said before, the long jump is a learned art and I believe Johnny's jumps would get much better with practice.

Chapter 25

Ted was allowing Johnny to run some races on the track with his athletes. This would give Johnny the feel of the actual race with other competitors. The young boys welcomed it. As a matter of fact, Johnny had already formed some friendships. And let me tell you, these boys knew how fast Johnny was.

I would not allow Johnny to cut it all the way loose on the 100 or the quarter. I thought that would be kinda like braggin'. So, Johnny always dialed it back a bit. But he got the taste of the race. AND HE LIKED IT.

He became good friends with a shy young man by the name of Charley Buckland. He had a little Indian blood in him and was one of the fastest sprinters on the team. They became training partners and I believe Johnny picked up some pointers from Charley that I could not provide.

I was shooting for the National Championships coming up in June. They were to be held in St. Louis, Missouri.

Now the National Championships are not where most athletes usually start their careers. But Johnny was different. And with my recommendation and that of Ted's, our entry was accepted. The three musketeers were going to take another road trip.

Chapter 26

St. Louis was a nice town. A little too big for my taste. Johnny had allowed Kathy to set us up at an exclusive hotel downtown. I had Johnny entered in the 100-yard dash and also the quarter mile. At that time, the events in the National Championships were measured in yards or the American system of measurement. In the Olympics, the metric system was used.

Johnny breezed through the preliminaries at both events. I told him to hold back and just make sure he got second or third place in order to advance to the finals.

On the day of the finals, the quarter mile was the first event of the two and was held at about 10 a.m. Kathy leaned over the railing of the stands and gave Johnny a kiss on the cheek and said, "Run, Johnny, run."

I just said, "Good luck, son."

The wind was recorded at 1.5 mph, which was within the limit to be a record.

Johnny got an extremely good start and led the whole race. He still had fairly long black hair but it was not as long as when I met him. (Kathy had convinced him to get it cut some.) It took some doing as long hair is a tradition in his Native American culture. But he was a picture to watch and a hush fell over the stadium. At the 220-yard split, Johnny's time was 22.4 seconds. It was a blistering pace and he had already left the field way behind by the halfway point of the race.

Kathy was screaming so loud that I thought that my ear drums were going to explode.

Johnny kept up that pace through the final turn and then turned on the burners at the start of the final straightaway. I'd seen him do it so many times but it was special seeing him do it in competition for the first time. Real competition. These were the finest runners of the day in this race but Johnny just left them in the dust.

He crossed the finish line with a time of 44.6 seconds. Three tenths of a second under the current world record. He was now the world record holder in the quarter mile. I just felt like shoutin', "I told ya so."

Johnny made a bee line for Kathy after the race. He hugged her and she started crying. Everyone in the stadium knew that they had witnessed something very special that day. I was elated but I had a weird sad sensation that now my secret was out to the world. It was kinda neat to be the only one who knew the Johnny secret. Now the world would want to know everything about this young man.

Later that day came the final of the 100-yard dash. Johnny was showing signs of extreme fatigue after the quarter mile final. His muscles were twitching in his legs. It was definitely the very hardest that I had ever seen him run and his level of fatigue showed it.

The race was set to run at about 4:30 in the afternoon which gave Johnny only about six and a half hours to rest between races. A man named John Stearns had set a new world record for this race in the preliminaries with a time of 9.1 seconds.

Chapter 27

Johnny got off to a very slow start and I could tell right away that his fatigue was just too much to overcome. He finished in sixth place. Out of the medals. The precious race that day had just taken too much out of him. And that taught me something about Johnny that day.

John Stearns finished in first place with another time of 9.1 seconds. It was also a world-record time but only his time of 9.1 in the preliminaries was accepted as a world record.

Johnny was interviewed after the meet that day and in watching the interview later, I would say he handled himself quite well. He was still his soft-spoken self but when it got down to it, he had a very intelligent and articulate personality. He knew that he had entered a new chapter in his life that day.

We had a grand celebration that evening at the hotel and the three of us did partake in some very tasty champagne. Kathy insisted that we have the best. I had never tasted the best before and it's a good thing that I was not rich. I could get used to drinking champagne that tasted that good.

The drive back to Austin was very upbeat but uneventful. My head was spinning thinking about the finals.

Chapter 28

When we got back to Austin, Kathy told Johnny that she wanted to meet his family. She knew Johnny well enough to know that he was homesick. So, she called her father and he made reservations for a flight for them. He even set up, through a friend of his, for a car to pick them up at the airport. It seemed that Kathy had a good relationship with her father. Evidently, he doted on her.

Whatever she wanted, she got.

Myself… Well, I got a little fishing done while they were gone. There were a number of great lakes around Austin. Ted managed to get away for one day. It was like old times.

I had two offers come in for head coaching positions. It seems the word was out that I was coaching Johnny and his world record performance was, let's say, the talk of the town around the track and field community. I just told them that I would think about it.

It was nice to be considered and both offers were from prestigious universities and both salaries were far higher than my previous salary at the University of Minnesota.

I must admit that it kind of puffed my chest out a bit. And it gave me some satisfaction as I thought of the dean and the board at my former employer. I hoped they felt stupid. But I wasn't about to take an offer and let Johnny down. We were headed to the Olympics in Tokyo next year.

Chapter 29

When Kathy and Johnny returned, they (Kathy) recounted every detail of their trip.

"Johnny's mother is absolutely the most precious, wise, beautiful, and interesting woman that I have ever met," Kathy said enthusiastically. *Of course, I already knew that,* I thought. She went on and on and on about all of Johnny's brothers and sisters—how wise they were for their ages and how much fun she had with them.

When we returned to our workouts, I had decided to make some changes to Johnny's routine. The nationals made me think that Johnny needed to build more strength in his legs and overall endurance. So, we did a lot more timed runs at far closer intervals. Also, I had Johnny put in a lot more miles to build basic endurance. Johnny did not seem to mind. He trusted my decisions completely. I also sighed us up for a meet coming up in August. The new training regimen was designed to get Johnny better prepared for running multiple races on the same day or with not many days between races.

Kathy returned to her training with the women's team. She also was starting to keep a more rigorous schedule. They were both going through learning how to deal with the small injuries and nagging hurts that come along with the track and field sport. Sometimes I would hear them lamenting each other on their aches and pains like a couple of old people. Nothing against old people.

Johnny was making great progress in the long jump and I figured it was time for him to compete in the next meet.

Then one day after training, I noticed that Johnny was walking strange so I asked him what was wrong. He pointed to the front part of his lower leg and said it was staring to hurt pretty bad. Uh oh. Shin splints.

Shin splints are a very painful and debilitating condition where the tissue attached to the shin bone becomes unattached or loose. It comes from the pounding down of the legs on hard surfaces. It also comes when workouts are accelerated too fast, which is what I just did with Johnny. Boy, did I feel like a heel! I had let Johnny down. I let my desire to succeed cloud my judgment. And shin splints usually take four to six weeks to heal. And they come right back if you start to train again before they are fully healed.

There was not much that could be done about shin splints except stay off it and put icepacks on it. Johnny and I had a lot of time on our hands. We visited the library at the university quite often.

I found some material on a very special person. I wanted Johnny to learn some about the great Jim Thorpe. He was the first Native American to win a gold medal in the Olympics. Johnny had not even heard of him. The reason being that a lot of comparisons were being made between himself and Jim Thorpe.

Jim Thorpe won the pentathlon and the decathlon in the 1912 Olympic Games in Stockholm, Sweden.

After Johnny finished reading the material that I gave him, I asked him what he thought.

"He was a great man but I think that I'm better looking than he was," Johnny said with a grin.

I just about fell down laughing when Johnny said that I certainly expected a more profound observation. Johnny rarely tried his hand at humor. But when he did, you could count on it being one of the funniest things you ever heard.

Chapter 30

Kathy, Johnny, and I attended all the meets that were held that year at the university—both the men's and the women's.

Charley Buckland, Johnny's friend, was having a great year. He was competing in the 100 and 220-yard dash and had placed second and third a number of times. Johnny did not like the 220 distances. He described it as too short to get my legs stretched out too long to really give it hell.

Another development was that Johnny and Charley were becoming best friends. Charley was including Johnny in on gatherings and introducing him to a lot of students at the university. Kathy told me that Johnny had told her that he had never really had a best or real close friend back home. Charley's friendship was very important to Johnny. I could see him growing as a person as he formed more acquaintances and friendships. He actually talked sometimes other than just answering a question.

Chapter 31

November came and it was a dark and terrible month. Nothing to do with us per say. The track and field season was over. We obviously didn't compete in the meet that I had signed Johnny up for. Johnny's leg was all healed.

But we received the news recently the same as the rest of the country. John Fitzgerald Kennedy, our president, had been assassinated in Dallas, Texas.

It was one of the few times in my adult life that I cried. People were crying everywhere you went. Like I say, it was a dark and terrible month.

How could anybody do such a horrible thing? And the people here in Texas seemed to almost have a shared guilt since it happened here in our state. Almost as if we were somehow partially to blame as it happened in our state, which was ridiculous. Monsters such as the man who committed this heinous act have shown up throughout history.

We were now the four musketeers, with the addition of Charley, and we attended the local

Presbyterian Church that following Sunday. It's all we could think of to do. I have never been a very religious man and have never really attended church regularly. But attending church and praying with others at this time seemed like the right thing to do.

Johnny and Kathy actually started attending church fairly regularly after that time. It seems to me that this is how religion and faith work. We are drawn to our faith in our time of need.

I of course remained too hard headed to attend church regularly. I, by the way, do believe in a higher power. I just don't believe in worrying about it too much, or talking about it all the time for that matter.

Chapter 32

Christmas was upon us again, and Kathy was decorating our little cabin like Santa was coming or something. Of course, if you believe in Santa Claus, as I do, then it was justified.

Now let me say at this point and it is very important—to me that is. I was happier during this time than I had ever been in my entire life. My relationship with Johnny and Kathy was far more than the business of coaching two talented athletes. I would like to think that I had grown as a person since meeting both of them. They had both gotten really deep under my skin.

I was sitting around the cabin a few days before Christmas when I heard Kathy's bug come screeching up out front.

"Come with me right now, Ralph," Kathy belted out. "Something's going on with Johnny." Then she grabbed me by the arm and yanked me out the front door.

As she spun, gravel leaving the house, she started to explain to me what she had heard.

"Johnny is involved in something over at the Cottington Manor."

"What do you mean involved?" I said.

"I don't know anything except that Johnny and I know quite a few people who live there," Kathy replied. "Charley used to live there," she added.

We were blazing down the road in her little car. Just then, we saw flashing lights up ahead. As we approached a parking lot, we saw a crowd of people next to the three-story apartment building.

We could see police officers everywhere but no sign of Johnny. Then Kathy spotted a girl she knew who lived in the apartments and rushed over to talk to her. A few minutes later, she rushed back over to me and said, "Let's go, Ralph."

So, we headed down the road, again at break-neck speed.

"So, what's up?" I finally said.

"The police have taken Johnny downtown for questioning. He evidently broke through a police barrier, ran up three flights of stairs, and rescued a girl that was being held at gunpoint!" Kathy exclaimed in bewilderment.

Whoa! I should have guessed that one. Foolishly, my first thought was that Johnny had gotten in a fight or something foolish as young people do. Even the best of them sometimes. I had forgotten the stories that Johnny's mother and Flo had told me about Johnny.

"Evidently, Johnny entered the apartment building, ran up three flights of stairs, climbed out on a ledge, entered the apartment next to the one where the man was holding the girl, entered the room somehow, tackled the man, threw the gun out the window, and struggled with the man until the police came up and took him away. Now the police have taken Johnny to the station for questioning. And that's where we're going," she said.

It occurred to me that Kathy did not have any knowledge about this side of her boyfriend. It hadn't occurred to me to tell her that Johnny was a bona fide hero back home on multiple occasions. And Johnny sure wasn't going to tell her.

Chapter 33

When we got to the station, Johnny was still filling out some papers at a desk. Kathy bolted for Johnny like a rocket and almost knocked him out of the chair. It was a combination of what were you thinking and I love you, I love you, I love you, etc.

I walked up to the detective and introduced myself and asked him what had happened. He explained that the paperwork was just routine. He was being KIND and not charging Johnny for not obeying the officer who was guarding the door. And ACKNOWLEDGED that Johnny had indeed done their job for them in disarming and detaining the suspect while not even harming him until the police got there. Thereby probably saving the young girls life. But I told myself, *this man is just doing his job.*

The newspaper reporters and flashing cameras greeted us as we exited the police station. From that moment on, all three of our lives were different. It was on the front page of every major newspaper in the country the following day.

"World record holder rescues woman." And various combinations of that.

Johnny was interviewed and of course he was humble about the encounter.

Now the world knew both of Johnny's secrets. He is one of the fastest men who ever lived and a bona fide hero to boot.

Many of the things that were written about Johnny Were such a contrast between a man like Johnny and a man like Oswald, who only last month assassinated one of the greatest men who ever lived—John Fitzgerald Kennedy, almost like a redemption for the human race.

And like I said, Johnny's life was never the same. In that, he could no longer go anywhere and not be recognized and people would fawn all over him.

Now some men would just love that, at least at first. But Johnny was devastated by this treatment. It was quite an adjustment for him.

It wasn't the same for Kathy or me either. Word got out to the press that we called ourselves 'the three musketeers' and what a hullabaloo they made over that.

Chapter 34

So, there was never a time again when Johnny trained that the stands were not full. And I had a new job. I now was not just Johnny's coach. Now I was also his agent and mediator between him and the press and many companies and agencies vying for his time. So, when I say things were different. I mean DIFFERENT.

It was so overwhelming at first that I could not sleep at night. I think all three of us were having trouble sleeping. But we eventually learned how to deal with it and returned to our routines.

Kathy's mother and father were summoned by Kathy. They came out after the first of the year. They rented a suite downtown big enough to handle the two of them and an adjoining suite for their lawyers. We needed the help in that regard and they were here to take over Johnny's BUSINESS. Yes, and he had become a business at that point.

He was receiving some of the largest offers for endorsements seen to that date. I certainly didn't have any talent for handling those sorts of affairs. So,

Johnny and I trusted them completely to do Johnny's bidding.

I was very fond of Kathy's parents and in talking to them many times, they expressed their remorse for not giving Kathy more love and attention when she was younger. But I do not think that Kathy was bitter. I think the reason for that was that both her parents definitely loved her very much. I guess that love stuff can take you pretty far.

Chapter 35

So eventually, a contract was written up for the arrangement between Johnny and me. Of course, Johnny wanted to just let me handle it.

"I trust you completely, Ralph," Johnny said to me.

But I insisted that he be directly involved in the process. So, I won't go into the details but we ended up with a fair agreement.

We finally began focusing on training again and it was quite a relief for the three of us.

Kathy had begun classes as the second semester began. Let me say at this point that she was no longer the gum-smacking smart aleck that I first met. She did very well in school, which, from what I understand, was 180 degrees from how she did in high school.

As Johnny and I resumed his training, I had a new plan. We talked it over and were agreed on the plan. Johnny performed his absolute best when given optimum time in between races and competition. We would train steady but no longer train HARD Instead of striving for better strength and stamina to run more races closer together. We would just keep Johnny extremely fit and ready for competition. But just make sure that there was plenty of time between competition and races.

Year 1964 was a whirlwind. I was a bit like Johnny in that I resented all the imposition on my privacy and all the attention we were getting.

We would focus again on the U.S. National Track and Field Championships. They were to be held this year on June 26 to 28 in New Brunswick, N.J. Johnny would finally be entered in the long jump. His first time in competition. Also, the 100-meter dash. Last year, Johnny had competed in the quarter mile and the 100-yard dash. This year, he was to compete in the 100-meter dash and the long jump. The governing bodies had changed the measuring system from American Standard to the Metric standard of measurements for the events.

I was not going to make the same mistake again so he was not entered into the 400-meter race. Of course, he already held the world record for the 440 yard or quarter of a mile event.

Again, Johnny breezed through the preliminary races but he was not faring well in the long jump. He had only one legal jump. He was having trouble getting his steps right on the approach. So, on the final day of the meet, I scratched him from the event. Then he could concentrate on the 100 meters.

A man named John Stearns was also in the final that day. He was the current world record holder in the event.

As race time approached, I told Johnny, "Just remember what advice Kathy gave you just before the quarter last year—Run, Johnny, run." He laughed.

Johnny had an average start out of the blocks. I believe he was in about third place after about 20 meters. Then it started. The burners. They came on. At about the halfway point of the race, Johnny was about a yard behind the leader, John Stearns, who had the burners on too.

It was absolute poetry in motion. Johnny gained ground about an inch at a time until at the finish line they were neck and neck as they crossed the line.

John Stearns had nudged Johnny out for the win with a time of 10.3. It was so close that Johnny also had a time of 10.3. WHAT A RACE!

Chapter 36

We would now focus on the upcoming Olympics to be held in Tokyo, Japan, in October. And the Olympic Trials.

Johnny's friend Charley Buckland was working with Johnny on his start for the 100 meters. His strengths were the opposite of Johnny's when it comes to the sprints. Charley had a tremendous take off. When we saw him race, he would sometimes be in first place by three yards in the first 20 yards of the race. It was a great advantage. His high-end speed just wasn't there. Johnny on the other hand was one of the ones three yards behind at the start of the race. But his high-end speed was unmatched. So, if he could just improve his start. Well, you get the picture.

The key was staying low coming out of the blocks. Charley had it down. Johnny's reaction time was good. He just needed to really work on staying low out of the blocks and really using his leg strength with each step.

Charley was a master at teaching Johnny and his start improved exponentially after working with Charley.

It was Charley's senior year and he was again having a very good season. He even managed to place first in the 100-yard dash against my old school, the University of Minnesota.

I took us all out to dinner to celebrate that one. Oh, and by the way, endorsement money was coming in and Johnny's bank account and mine were blossoming.

Johnny of course sent almost all the money back home to his mother. He kept just enough as needed to get by.

Kathy was doing very well in school and was competing in the women's track and field. She only cared about one event—the 880. And let me tell ya. We were right about her too.

In her first meet, she had a respectable time. Then her time improved each meet for the entire season. She placed second twice and in the final meet of the year, she took first place.

I was just kinda pinching myself at that point, thinking, *has any other track and field coach in history been this blessed? I don't think so.*

Chapter 37

Now I need to mention at this point that all of this could not have happened without the help of my friend, Ted. And let me tell ya. Ted and I were like two proud grandpas when it came to Johnny and Kathy. I felt that Ted was as important to their success as I was.

In the upcoming months, Johnny and I would have to travel first to Randal's Island, New York. And then to Los Angeles, California, for the Olympic Trials. Kathy stayed behind to concentrate on her school work and track.

Now Johnny was no fan of airline travel. In fact, I had to use every trick in my book to coax him into boarding the plane.

What worked the best was that I concocted a story about a great bird we might encounter on the flight. In other words, think of Johnny like you would a very young child. Which he was in some ways. Very innocent. Johnny saw for the first time the ultra-metropolitan cities of New York and Los Angeles. I think that it made him sad to see humanity on that scale. I know because after we returned home to Austin after the trials, Johnny and I had a heart-to-heart talk.

He said to me, "Ralph, I really appreciate everything that you have done for me. And I look forward to competing in the Olympics in Tokyo. But win or lose, I am going home after that. To stay."

"OK," I said. "I will respect your wish, Johnny."

Chapter 38

Johnny did quite well in the Olympic Trials. He qualified easily for the 100 meters, 400 meters, and the long jump. In the 100 meters in Los Angeles, Johnny's time was 10.2 seconds. It was his best time to date. And it was the same time that Jesse Owens had to win gold in the 1936 Olympics in Germany—in front of Hitler.

The summer Olympics were to be held October 10 through October 24 in Tokyo, Japan.

Johnny and I got to the Olympic village in late September. Now you talk about culture shock. For both of us, the frenzy of that city that we witnessed on our ride from the airport was mind-bending. For both of us.

We had no desire to leave the village.

Kathy came out later with her folks right before the finals. Daddy Joe, or Joe Murphy, had been to Tokyo on business multiple times and knew his way around the city quite well. They stayed in a hotel fairly near the village. They did take in some of the sights in Tokyo and Kathy had many memories of the trip. Her fondest memory, she told me later, was the quality of the time she spent with her parents. It's never too late to SHOW someone how much you love them.

Chapter 39

The final in the 100 meters was held on October 15. Johnny was in Lane 3. John Stearns, the current record holder in the event, was in Lane 5.

Kathy and her parents were in the stands next to me. We were about four rows up near the finish line.

I was nervous as a cat in a room full of rocking chairs.

Johnny seemed to be handling the pressure of the competition better than I was. In fact, it amazed me how cool he was under pressure.

BANG! The gun sounded and they were off. Johnny got his best start ever and he led the race start to finish. Kathy again almost burst my eardrums screaming and I got so excited that I almost fell forward on to an elderly couple.

Johnny absolutely blistered the track, start to finish. It seemed to me that he just ran faster and faster during the entire race. He finished almost a full stride ahead of John Stearns, the second-place finisher.

John Stearns' time was 10.0 seconds, which tied the world record. Johnny's time was 9.8 seconds, which was a new world record and an Olympic record also.

What I noticed as a coach was that Johnny seemed fresh as a daisy after the race, which was extremely good news because the final in the long jump and the 400 meters were coming up in just a couple of days.

I think that Johnny was getting stronger and more resilient as far as running races with minimum rest. He had run quite a few races in the past few days in the qualifying heats.

The long jump final was held on October 18. Johnny had one very good jump a few days earlier in the qualifying rounds. That jump was about five inches farther than his previous best.

I had taken note of one thing that another jumper was doing and had initiated it into Johnny's approach and jump.

I first noticed it and pointed it out to Johnny. The jumper was Phil Johnson and he was the current World Record holder in the event. It had to do with his arm swing and arm thrust at the point of takeoff.

During the finals, everything was working for Johnny. He did not foul even once. Every jump was very good. His longest jump was his second jump and it earned him first place in the event. It was also a new Olympic and World Record. The jump was measured at 27 feet, eight and a quarter inch, a full four inches farther than the current World Record.

It was a monumental accomplishment and Johnny always treasured it as his finest achievement. I believe because it was such a long process to learn and refine his approach and leap. Running to Johnny just came so easy that it did not seem like as much of an accomplishment to excel in the running events. I had to agree.

Team USA was disappointed that I did not allow Johnny to compete in the relays but I had two reasons.

One: I knew of Johnny's limits as far as competing with limited rest. I think it had to do with just how much Johnny pushed his own limits when he ran.

Two: Most of the competitors had run relay races on multiple occasions during high school and college. Johnny did not have that experience and practice. The passing of the baton can be a tricky thing. And it can be even trickier if you have never done it before.

Chapter 40

The final in the 400 meters was held the next day.

This was my personal favorite that Johnny competed in. Maybe it was because it was at this distance that I first witnessed Johnny's ability.

BANG! They were off. Johnny again led the race wire to wire. There was an absolute cacophony of cheers of Johnny, Johnny, Johnny coming from the stands.

Approaching the halfway point of the race or 200 meters, Johnny was leading by a ridiculous margin. I was very worried that he would burn out at such a pace. At the 200 split, Johnny had a time of 22.4 seconds. I really believed at the time that even as good as Johnny was that this pace was just TOO FAST.

As Johnny rounded the curve, he had held the pace that he was keeping. Even as his coach, I just couldn't imagine that he could keep up this pace any longer.

I WAS WRONG.

Johnny made his classic move where he lowers his head just a little and puts the pedal to the metal. And as impossible as it seemed to me, he turned the speed up even more to the finish line.

Johnny had won the 400 meters in a time of 44 seconds even. A new Olympic Record. And a new World Record. It was an absolute magnificent and almost inhuman performance.

Chapter 41

The first thing that we did when we returned home was that we rented a couple of suites downtown. We were now all occupying the entire sixth floor of the posh hotel that Kathy's parents were staying in.

The amount of publicity that Johnny received for his accomplishments in the Olympics was gargantuan. We simply could not continue to live in our cozy little cabin.

Joe Murphy began to handle all of our affairs.

Kathy continued to excel in her studies but all the attention that the three of us received made it hard to concentrate sometimes.

The plan was to stay just a couple weeks or so and then drive the old boat back to South Dakota. I had promised Johnny. Only this time we would not be accompanied by our chatty back seat companion.

Kathy stayed on in Austin to continue her studies and she eventually bought a nice house on the outskirts of town.

So this time the road trip was drab without Kathy, our captain. Many people recognized Johnny along the way and he was introduced to the art of the autograph.

He signed heads, yearbooks, hats, and various body parts.

You name it. He was congenial for the process.

Again, the whole trip was spent in the front seat for Johnny, my faithful shotgun rider.

He was going to be returning home a hero. I wondered how it would feel to Johnny when he saw any of the mean young men who had chastised him before.

Now I'm sure that Johnny's mindset was much different than mine. If it was me I would blow a trumpet as loud as I could right in their face. Johnny just shook their hand and greeted them with as much warmth as any other person in town.

Johnny's heart was every bit as big a wonder as his athletic accomplishments.

Chapter 42

I stayed in town for a few days at the motel that I had stayed in before. And got some o' that blueberry pie off a Flo at the Wagon Wheel.

Of course, I had to tell Flo every detail of what happened since Johnny's departure. Flo and I had dinner one night at the other (better) restaurant in town. I sprang.

And then there was the parade for Johnny. It was quite fitting that one of the (floats) in the parade was the buckboard that started this whole adventure. With the little girl (older now) riding shotgun. It took me back.

I was extremely happy for Johnny but I knew it was really the end of my coaching career. That made me a tiny bit sad.

I was a dinner guest at the white residence for a couple of nights. And I found out where Johnny got his cooking skills.

Johnny's mother was an absolutely fabulous cook. Along with her apprentice, who was the world champion at three-track and field events.

I had been fairly thin for my entire life. But I seriously doubt that I could maintain that status if I were to stick around there much longer.

Kathy's mother and father moved back to their home in California and Joe went on handling all of Johnny's business affairs.

Johnny ended up with two of the largest product endorsements of the day. Adidas shoes and Wheaties, the breakfast cereal. Johnny was seen on the front of one of America's favorite breakfast cereals for years to come.

Me you ask. What did I do? Oh, I jumped in the boat and headed it to Florida. My sister had come to the conclusion that I might not have been crazy after all. And I was looking forward to seeing my sister and my brother in-law.

My sister has a heart of gold. And she is very protective when it comes to me, her only brother and only sibling.

When I got there, I was received as a hero. My sister and my brother in-law had been braggin' me up all over town. So it was quite easy for me to make new friendships.

It looked like a good time to enjoy some of the best fishing waters known to man.

I stayed at my sister's for about a month. Then I rented a little seaside flat with a garage and a workshop. I didn't know how to build anythin'. But maybe I could learn.

The three musketeers spent that Christmas in our separate locations but we stayed in touch extensively.

Chapter 43

It was late March in 1965 when I received a call from Johnny. He had set up a college fund for each of his brothers and sisters. And the big news was that Johnny had purchased a ranch for himself and his family—and not on the reservation.

Johnny described the ranch as real pretty but a functioning horse ranch. Johnny wanted to raise horses. I remembered now his mother telling me about his love for horses and his talent for training them. I was thrilled for him and I assured him that I would make it out real soon and see the place.

Now the next thing that I have to report is not good news. Shortly after I moved to my flat, my sister caught my brother-in-law cheating on her. And she was devastated. My sister had a kind of a delicate psyche anyway and I would say that she was the least equipped person to handle such a thing. And her love for John was great. And John was great. But evidently, some pretty little blond that lived down the street thought so too.

It turned out that my move to Florida was very well timed. My sister needed me through this and I was so glad that I was there for her. It hit her real hard. And it was very hard for me to not show my resentment for John when I saw him, which was unfortunate since I had been looking forward to sharing times with him. That wasn't gonna happen now. I could not hide my feelings.

Chapter 44

Johnny went on to raise and train some of the finest horses for breeding and for racing.

After the school year was over, Kathy came out to spend the summer with Johnny at the ranch. Johnny asked her to marry him. She said, "Sure, cowboy."

The wedding was to be held in July. I flew out for the ceremony. So did Kathy's parents. Charley Buckland also flew out for the ceremony and was Johnny's best man.

The night of the ceremony, we had a huge bonfire and much libation and a live band. I think you could probably see that bonfire from space. A good time was had by many. And I absolutely cherished my time visiting with Terry, Johnny's mother.

I had many fine memories of my time with a couple of the most wonderful friends a man could have. It was a magical time. That's the only way that I can describe it.

After Johnny asked Kathy to marry her, she sold her house in Austin and moved to the ranch. They became Mr. and Mrs. White. Kathy became quite a cowgirl.

Johnny had great success with the horses that he acquired. And he became known as one of the best horse trainers in the business. From what I understand, a fellow rancher had a very well-bred but high-spirited horse that nobody could work with. Johnny bought him for a bargain price. After working with him for a year, he did well on the thoroughbred circuit. So well that Johnny entered him in the Kentucky Derby. And guess who took first place? It turned out that the fastest man who ever lived also had an eye for that talent in horses.

The End